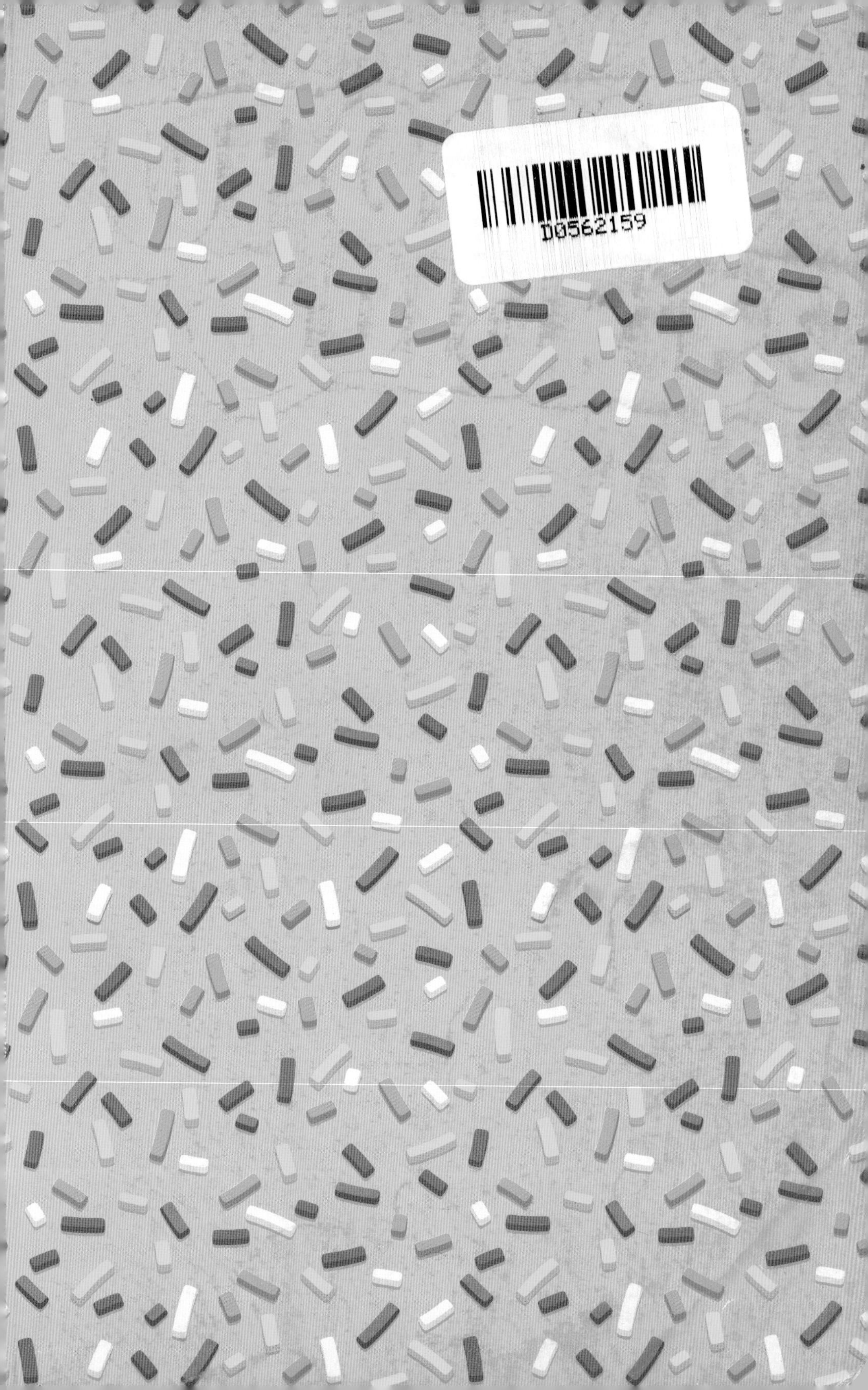
D0562159

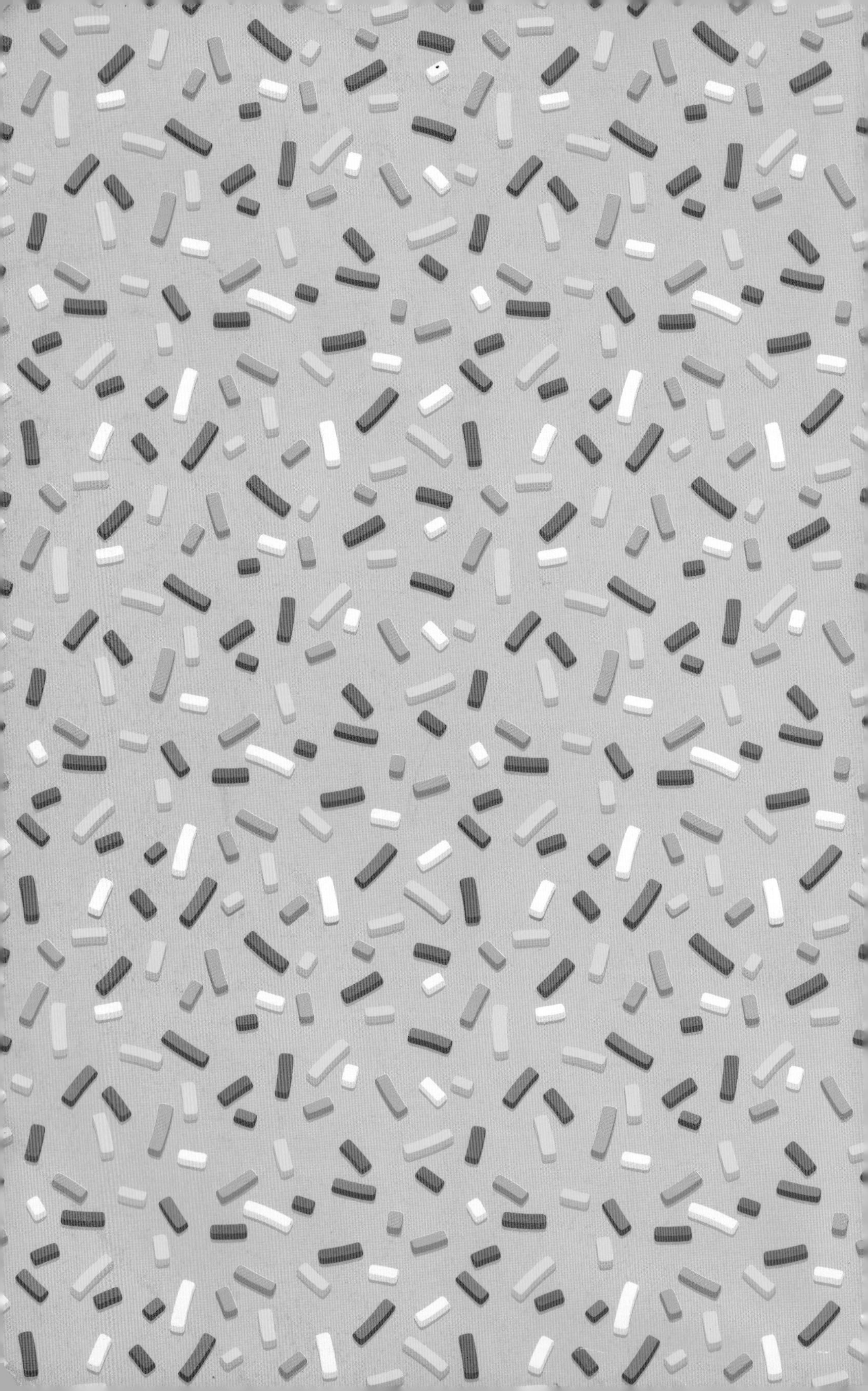

Katie and the Cupcake Cure

This book is a work of fiction. Any references to historical events, real people, or real places are used fictitiously. Other names, characters, places, and events are products of the author's imagination, and any resemblance to actual events or places or persons, living or dead, is entirely coincidental.

SIMON SPOTLIGHT
An imprint of Simon & Schuster Children's Publishing Division
1230 Avenue of the Americas, New York, New York 10020
This Simon Spotlight edition August 2022
Copyright © 2022 by Simon & Schuster, Inc.
All rights reserved, including the right of reproduction in whole or in part in any form.
SIMON SPOTLIGHT and colophon are registered trademarks of Simon & Schuster, Inc.
For information about special discounts for bulk purchases, please contact Simon & Schuster Special Sales at 1-866-506-1949 or business@simonandschuster.com.
Text by Tracey West
Cover and Character Design by Manuel Preitano
Art by Giulia Campobello at Glass House Graphics
Assistant on inks by Marzia Migliori
Colors by Francesca Ingrassia
Lettering by Giuseppe Naselli/Grafimated Cartoon
Supervision by Salvatore Di Marco/Grafimated Cartoon
Designed by Laura Roode
The text of this book was set in Comic Crazy.
Manufactured in China 0522 SCP
10 9 8 7 6 5 4 3 2 1
ISBN 978-1-6659-1403-1 (hc)
ISBN 978-1-6659-1402-4 (pbk)
ISBN 978-1-6659-1404-8 (ebook)
Library of Congress Catalog Card Number 2022934414

Cupcake Diaries

Katie and the Cupcake Cure

By
Coco Simon

Illustrated by
Giulia Campobello
at Glass House Graphics

Simon Spotlight
New York London Toronto Sydney New Delhi

Katie Brown

Mia Vélaz-Cruz

Chapter 1

Dear diary,
Tomorrow is the first day of middle school. I should probably be nervous, but I'm not. Callie and I
BFF
LA DA DEE
06:30
SSSSSWISH!

HAPPY FIRST DAY OF MIDDLE SCHOOL, KATIE!
Dr. Brown
I MADE YOU A SPECIAL BREAKFAST!

MOM,YOU ARE THE MARTHA STEWART OF MAPLE GROVE.
MAYBE, BUT CAN MARTHA CLEAN YOUR TEETH AND FILL A CAVITY WITHOUT BREAKING A SWEAT?

DID YOU GET THE MAP I TEXTED YOU? WITH THE NEW BUS STOP?
DR. BROWN

YEAH, I GOT IT. I'M GOING TO MEET CALLIE ON RIDGE STREET, AND WE'RE WALKING THERE TOGETHER.

I HAVE TO GO SHOPPING WITH MY MOM.

AND WHEN SHE GOT BACK, SHE KEPT MAKING EXCUSES ABOUT WHY SHE COULDN'T SEE ME.

WE'D PROMISED THAT WE'D STICK TOGETHER. NO MIDDLE SCHOOL BLUES FOR US!

First Day of K

IT WAS WEIRD. CALLIE AND I WERE BEST FRIENDS. WE HAD GONE TO EVERY FIRST DAY OF SCHOOL TOGETHER.

SHE PROBABLY FORGOT TO CHARGE HER PHONE.
THERE'S A SURPRISE IN YOUR LUNCH.
I HOPE IT'S SOMETHING YUMMY AND NOT LIKE, EXPLODING CONFETTI.
DR. BROWN
GUESS YOU'LL FIND OUT AT LUNCHTIME.
LOVE YOU, KATIE!
LOVE YOU, TOO!
MIDDLE SCHOOL IS GOING TO BE AWESOME!

WHERE ARE YOU, CALLIE?

WHAT WAS CALLIE DOING WITH SYDNEY, MAGGIE, AND BRENDA? AND WHERE WERE CALLIE'S GLASSES?

HEY, CAL!

MAYBE SHE DOESN'T RECOGNIZE ME WITHOUT HER GLASSES.

HEY, THE BUS STOP'S THAT WAY!

YEAH, WE'RE, UM, WALKING TO SCHOOL.
BUT I THOUGHT WE WERE TAKING THE BUS.

ONLY LITTLE KIDS TAKE THE BUS.

NICE SHIRT, KATIE. DID YOU MAKE THAT AT CAMP?

HA HA HA HA HA

AS A MATTER OF FACT, I *DID* MAKE THIS AT CAMP.

COME ON. I DON'T WANT TO BE LATE.

CALLIE, WHAT IS GOING ON?

SHRUG

Chapter 2

VROOM!
SCHOOL BUS

CALLIE AND I WERE SUPPOSED TO SIT TOGETHER.

OKAY, SHE SEEMS NICE.

THANKS FOR THE SEAT!
NO PROBLEM.

SHE MUST HAVE GONE TO A DIFFERENT ELEMENTARY SCHOOL.
I'M KATIE.
MIA.

DID YOU GO TO RICHARDSON? I WENT TO HAMILTON.

I JUST MOVED HERE FROM MANHATTAN.

MIA FROM MANHATTAN. THAT'S EASY TO REMEMBER!
I SOUND LIKE SUCH A DORK!

I'VE BEEN TO MANHATTAN TO SEE *THE LION KING* ON BROADWAY. THE CITY WAS CROWDED AND REALLY NOISY AND...

MY NEIGHBORHOOD WAS PRETTY QUIET, ACTUALLY.
GREAT, I INSULTED HER!

I LIKE IT THERE. AND I STILL LIVE THERE, KIND OF. MY DAD DOES, ANYWAY.

ARE HER PARENTS DIVORCED, LIKE MINE?

BY THE WAY, I REALLY LIKE YOUR SHIRT. DID YOU MAKE IT?

UM, YEAH, AT CAMP.
THAT SOUNDS FUN! I THOUGHT CAMP WAS ALL HIKING AND CANOEING, UGH!
SHUDDER

PFSSSSSST

MY HOMEROOM IS IN 212. WHAT'S YOURS?

I CAN'T FIND IT! GO AHEAD WITHOUT ME.
ARE YOU SURE?
HOMEROOM 212

YEAH.

ARGH!

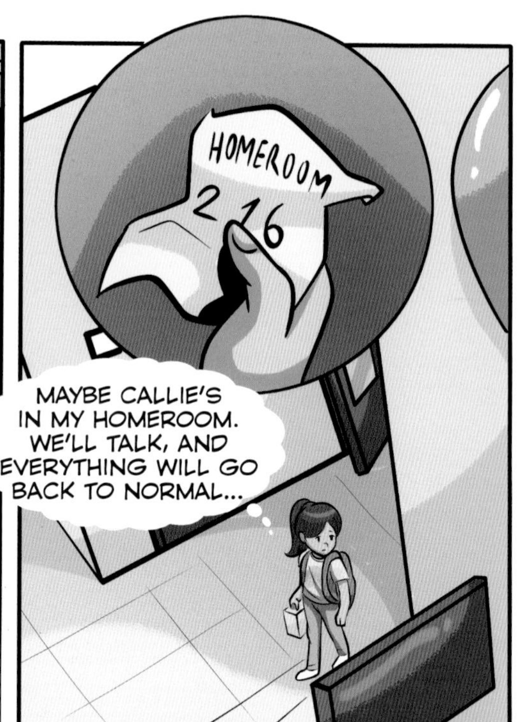
HOMEROOM
216
MAYBE CALLIE'S IN MY HOMEROOM. WE'LL TALK, AND EVERYTHING WILL GO BACK TO NORMAL...

CHATTER-CHATTER

NO CALLIE...

PGC

HEY, DO YOU KNOW IF CALLIE IS IN THIS HOMEROOM?

WHY DON'T YOU ASK HER YOURSELF?
GIGGLE

MAYBE MIDDLE SCHOOL ISN'T GOING TO BE AS AWESOME AS I THOUGHT...

Chapter 3

I'M MR. INSLEY, AND THIS ROOM WILL BE YOUR FIRST STOP EVERY MORNING...

TODAY I'VE GOT SOME TIPS FOR YOU...
WHAT DID MAGGIE MEAN BY THAT?
AND THERE'S A SHORTCUT THROUGH THE GYM...
BUT MORE IMPORTANTLY, WHY IS SHE ACTING LIKE SHE DOESN'T EVEN KNOW ME?
OPENING YOUR LOCKER CAN BE TRICKY...
I DON'T REMEMBER MAGGIE AND BRENDA AND SYDNEY ACTING SO MEAN. NOT TO ME, ANYWAY.
CELL PHONES MUST BE TURNED OFF...
AND WHY IS CALLIE ACTING LIKE SHE'S THEIR BESTIE OR SOMETHING?

What happened this morning? R u taking the bus home or walking again?
What happened this morning? R u taking the bus home or walking again?
Let's talk after.
What happened this morning? R u taking the bus home or walking again?
Let's talk after.
After what? Where r u now? Where is ur homeroom? Can we talk b4 class? I can.

KATIE BROWN, RIGHT?
GULP!

I THINK YOU MISSED THE PART ABOUT NOT USING YOUR CELL PHONE IN CLASS.
SORRY!

NORMALLY, I'D HAVE TO CONFISCATE YOUR PHONE, BUT SINCE IT'S THE FIRST DAY OF SCHOOL, CONSIDER THIS A WARNING.
NOD

BUSTED!

WHOOSH!
ROOM 216
TIME MACHINE
BZZZT!

COME ON!

26...14...5

CLICK!

YES!

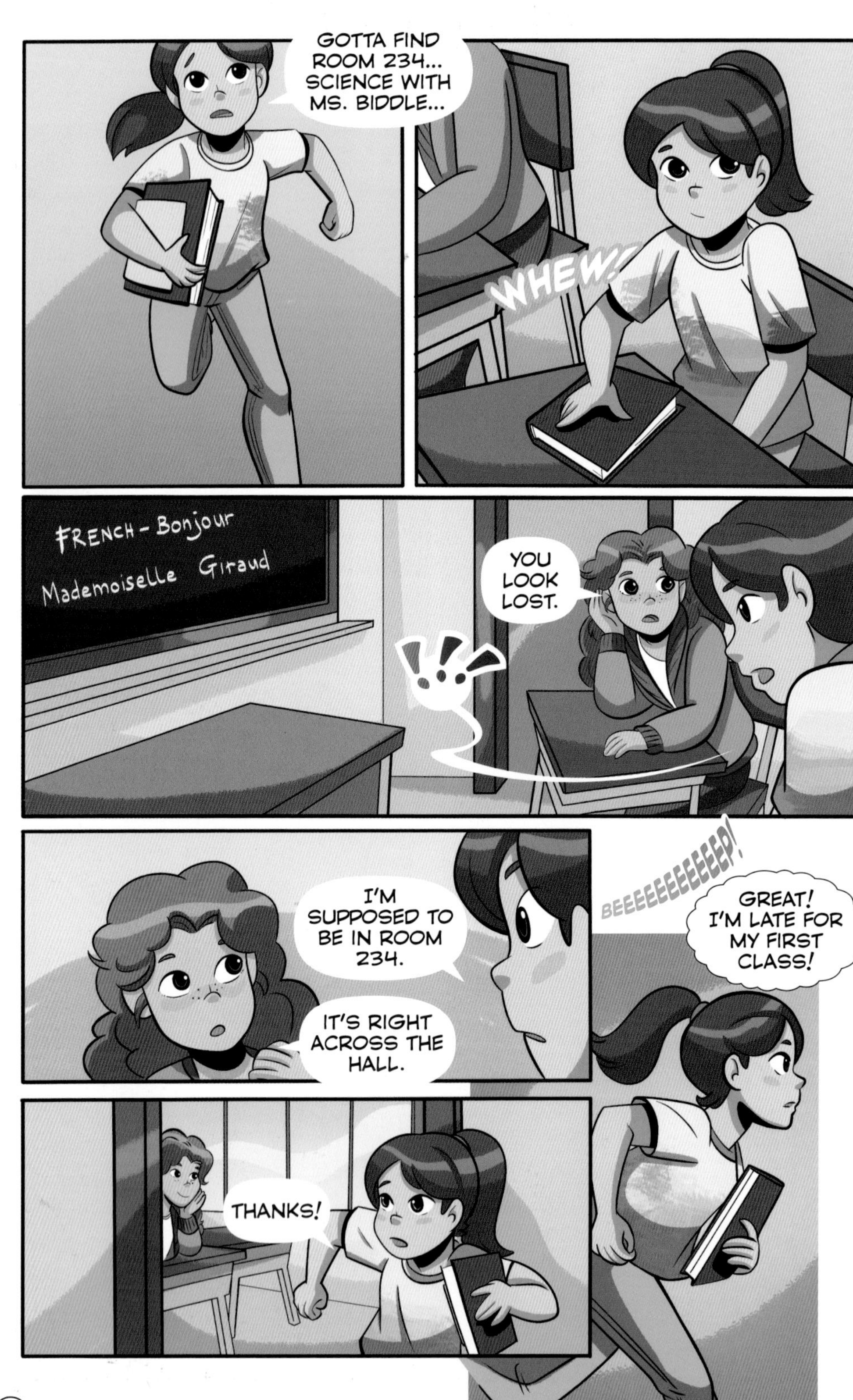
GOTTA FIND ROOM 234... SCIENCE WITH MS. BIDDLE...
WHEW!
FRENCH - Bonjour
Mademoiselle Giraud
YOU LOOK LOST.
!!
I'M SUPPOSED TO BE IN ROOM 234.
IT'S RIGHT ACROSS THE HALL.
BEEEEEEEEEEEEP!
GREAT! I'M LATE FOR MY FIRST CLASS!
THANKS!

Chapter 4

ENTER, ENTER, ALL YOU LOST SOULS!

I AM MS. BIDDLE, AND THIS IS MY CO-TEACHER, PRISCILLA.
OKAY, I'M NOT IN TROUBLE.

BASED ON THE PRESENCE OF PRISCILLA IN THE CLASSROOM...
...WHO CAN CREATE A HYPOTHESIS ABOUT WHAT WE'RE GOING TO LEARN THIS SEMESTER?

THE HUMAN BODY?

EXCELLENT! I CAN ALREADY TELL YOU'RE A BUNCH OF BRIGHT STUDENTS.

I CAN FEEL IT IN MY BONES...

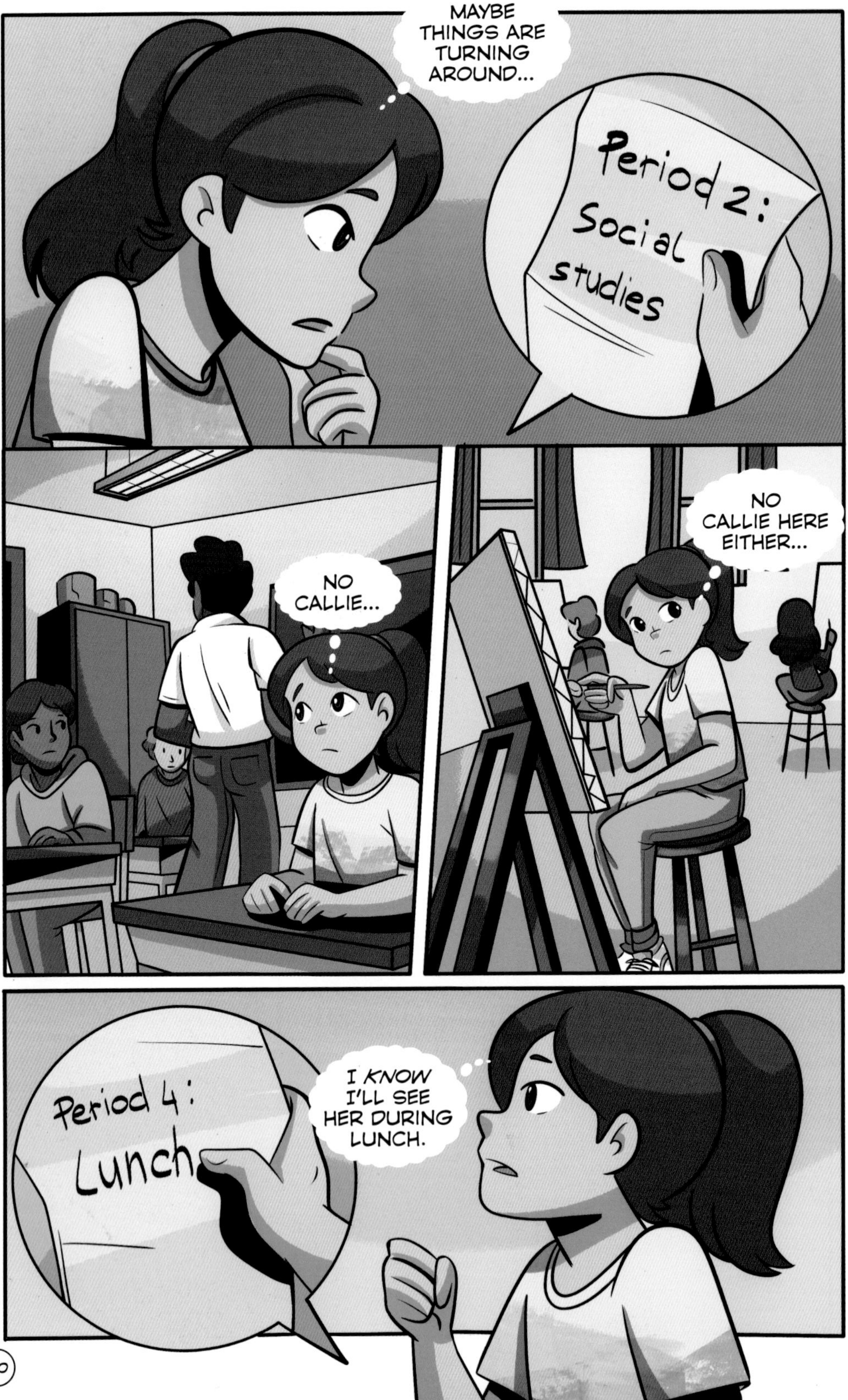

MAYBE THINGS ARE TURNING AROUND...

Period 2: Social studies

NO CALLIE...

NO CALLIE HERE EITHER...

SHE'S SAVED ME A SEAT!
SORRY, KATIE. THIS TABLE IS RESERVED FOR THE PGC.
PGC?
POPULAR. GIRLS. CLUB.
YOU HAVE TO BE A MEMBER TO SIT HERE. AND YOU ARE NOT.
?!

SO YOU'RE A MEMBER?
YEAH, IT'S NO BIG DEAL.

RIGHT. NO BIG DEAL.

I'LL SEE YOU LATER!

SIGH

A CUPCAKE
FOR MY
CUPCAKE

IS ANYONE SITTING HERE?
NO, UNLESS THEY'RE INVISIBLE.

HOW'S EVERYTHING GOING SO FAR?

LET'S SEE. I GOT INTO TROUBLE WITH MY HOMEROOM TEACHER. MY LOCKER HATES ME...

...AND MY BEST FRIEND WOULD RATHER HANG OUT WITH A BUNCH OF MEAN GIRLS THAN ME.

REALLY?

SADLY, IT'S ALL TRUE. HOW ABOUT YOU?

IT'S OKAY, JUST... DIFFERENT.
HEY, DO YOU HAVE MS. BIDDLE FOR SCIENCE? ISN'T SHE AWESOME?
YEAH, I LOVED HER SHIRT!

DO YOU WANT TO SIT HERE? THERE'S PLENTY OF ROOM.
THAT'S THE GIRL WHO HELPED ME EARLIER.
HI, I'M ALEXIS, AND THIS IS EMMA.
HI.
I'M KATIE.
AND I'M MIA.
DID YOU TWO GO TO RICHARDSON?
YES. DID YOU GO TO HAMILTON?
JUST KATIE. I'M FROM MANHATTAN.
OOH, I'VE ALWAYS WANTED TO GO THERE. WHAT'S IT LIKE?

ARE THEY LAUGHING ABOUT ME?

EARTH TO KATIE! I WAS ASKING YOU IF YOU HAD SOCIAL STUDIES YET.
OH, SORRY.

SHE'S A LITTLE OUT OF IT.
HER BEST FRIEND DUMPED HER TO HANG OUT WITH SOME MEAN GIRLS.

REALLY? WHICH ONES?
OH, I KNOW THOSE GIRLS FROM CAMP. YOU'RE RIGHT. THEY *ARE* MEAN.

I HONESTLY DON'T KNOW WHAT CALLIE'S DOING WITH THEM.

CALLIE'S YOUR FRIEND?

I THOUGHT CALLIE WAS VERY NICE.

THAT'S SO CUTE!

MY MOM PACKED IT FOR ME. SHE LOVES TO BAKE. I DO TOO.
YOUR MOM IS SO SWEET. WHAT KIND IS IT?

PEANUT BUTTER FROSTING WITH A LITTLE CINNAMON. AND GRAPE JELLY INSIDE.
SO IT'S A PB-AND-J CUPCAKE? COOL IDEA.

THERE'S A CUPCAKE SHOP IN MY DAD'S NEIGHBORHOOD THAT HAS FIFTY-SEVEN FLAVORS. I BET THEY HAVE PB-AND-J.

I FEEL WEIRD EATING THIS BY MYSELF. BUT IT'S TOO MESSY TO SHARE...

THE NEXT TIME MY MOM MAKES CUPCAKES, I'LL BRING SOME FOR ALL OF US.

COOL!
THANKS!
THANKS!

Chapter 5

GRUNT
YOU'RE LATE, MISS BROWN...
!!
BRING YOUR UNIFORM TOMORROW...
¡HOLA ESTUDIANTES!
OOF!

MY MOM WORKS FROM HOME, SO I GUESS I DON'T REALLY STAY HOME ALONE EITHER.

SEE YA!

BYE!

MOM SAID JOANNE HAS A RED CAR...

LOOKING FOR YOUR FORMER FRIEND?

HONK!
HONK!

HEY, KATIE! HOW WAS YOUR FIRST DAY?
UHHH...

DON'T WANT TO TALK ABOUT IT? THAT'S OKAY. I FEEL YOU, BUDDY.
JOANNE

RIIIIING!
RIIIIING!

HELLO?
CAN YOU TALK?
OF COURSE!
WHY DIDN'T YOU TELL ME WE WEREN'T TAKING THE BUS TOGETHER?
LISTEN, KATIE, I'M SORRY. I BECAME GOOD FRIENDS WITH SYDNEY, MAGGIE, AND BELLA AT CAMP.
BELLA? DON'T YOU MEAN BRENDA?
ANYWAY, THEY ASKED ME TO JOIN THEIR CLUB, AND I NEVER GOT A CHANCE TO TELL YOU.
YOU COULD HAVE CALLED ME OR TEXTED ME.
I KNOW, BUT I WAS JUST REALLY BUSY WHEN I GOT HOME. HONEST. PLEASE DON'T BE UPSET.

ARE WE STILL FRIENDS?
OF COURSE! YOU'RE MY BEST FRIEND!
ARE WE? BECAUSE YOU WOULDN'T EVEN EAT LUNCH WITH ME.
OR STAND UP FOR ME WHEN SYDNEY WAS BEING MEAN...

KATIE, WE'RE IN MIDDLE SCHOOL NOW. WE'RE BOTH GOING TO MAKE NEW FRIENDS. THAT'S NORMAL.

I'LL SEE YOU THIS WEEKEND FOR THE LABOR DAY BARBECUE.

HAVE YOU NOTICED I GOT CONTACT LENSES? NO MORE GLASSES FOR ME!
WELL, THAT EXPLAINS...

OOPS, ANOTHER CALL COMING IN. GOTTA GO!
BEEP

KATIE!

HOW WAS YOUR DAY? WERE YOUR TEACHERS NICE? DID YOU GET HOMEWORK?

DID YOU FIND THE BUS STOP OKAY? DID YOU LIKE THE CUPCAKE?

HEY, IT'S NICE OUT. WANT TO WALK OVER TO CALLIE'S WHEN WE'RE DONE?

UM, NO, I WAS THINKING... CAN WE MAKE PINEAPPLE UPSIDE-DOWN CUPCAKES INSTEAD?
TURN YOUR FROWN UPSIDE DOWN
OH, SO YOU NEED A CUPCAKE CURE?
DO YOU WANT TO TALK ABOUT IT?
WELL... MY LOCKER IS HARD TO OPEN.
YOU COULD ALWAYS ASK CALLIE FOR HELP.
UM... MAYBE...

OH, RIGHT, YOU SAID SHE'S NOT IN ANY OF YOUR CLASSES. THAT MUST BE TOUGH.
YOU DON'T EVEN KNOW!
TWENTY MINUTES LATER...
CAN I BRING FOUR WITH ME TOMORROW? FOR THE GIRLS AT MY LUNCH TABLE?
SURE! I HAVE A BOX YOU CAN USE.

Dear diary,
I'm still kind of in shock over what Callie did to me today. How can she say we're still best friends when she's not acting like a friend at all? I feel like I don't know how to act around her. Am I supposed to let her ignore me in school and talk to me only when Sydney, Maggie, and Bella aren't around?
I think if I hadn't met Mia, Emma, and Alexis, I would really be freaking out. I hope they still sit with me at lunch tomorrow. Mia is so cool that she'll probably make other friends. And I bet Emma and Alexis were just feeling sorry for me...
Katie

Chapter 6

THE NEXT DAY
IS THAT WHAT I THINK IT IS?
MY MOM AND I MADE SOME LAST NIGHT.
KATIE BROUGHT US CUPCAKES!
THAT'S SO NICE OF YOU!
I WAS JUST TELLING EMMA THAT MY FAMILY'S GOING DOWN THE SHORE THIS WEEKEND, FOR LABOR DAY. LAST SWIM OF THE SUMMER!
I'M GOING TO THE CITY, TO SEE MY DAD.
ARE YOUR PARENTS DIVORCED?
YEAH, FOUR YEARS AGO.
SHE SEES HER DAD ON WEEKENDS? I WONDER WHAT THAT'S LIKE.

THAT MUST BE HARD.
IT'S NOT A BIG DEAL. THEY'RE BOTH A LOT HAPPIER NOW.

ANYWAY, WHAT'S EVERYONE DOING THIS WEEKEND?
WE'RE GOING TO VISIT MY GRANDMA. KATIE, WHAT ABOUT YOU?

WE'RE GOING TO A BARBECUE OVER AT... CALLIE'S.

DIDN'T CALLIE DUMP YOU?
SHE DIDN'T DUMP ME. WE'RE STILL BEST FRIENDS.

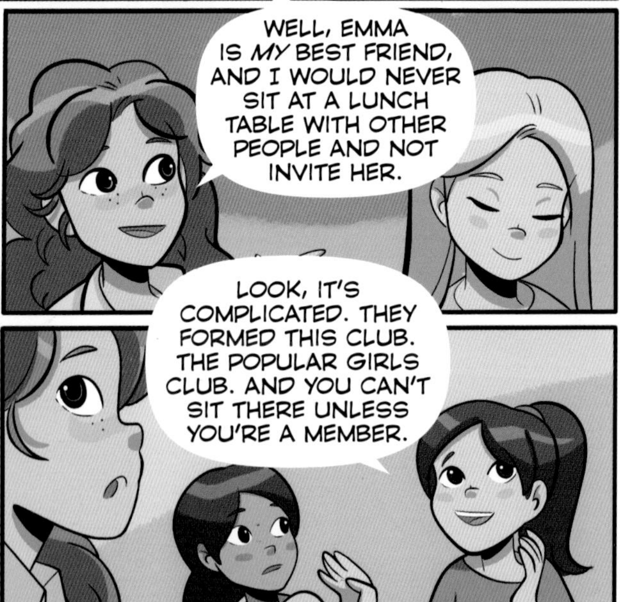
WELL, EMMA IS *MY* BEST FRIEND, AND I WOULD NEVER SIT AT A LUNCH TABLE WITH OTHER PEOPLE AND NOT INVITE HER.
LOOK, IT'S COMPLICATED. THEY FORMED THIS CLUB. THE POPULAR GIRLS CLUB. AND YOU CAN'T SIT THERE UNLESS YOU'RE A MEMBER.

ARE YOU SERIOUS? THEY ACTUALLY NAMED THEMSELVES THE "POPULAR GIRLS CLUB"? IF THEY'RE SO POPULAR, WHY DO THEY HAVE TO ADVERTISE IT?

IT *IS* A LITTLE DESPERATE. BUT I HAVE THOSE GIRLS IN A LOT OF MY CLASSES. THEY SEEM NICE.
CALLIE IS NICE. I'M NOT SO SURE ABOUT THE OTHERS.

IS IT CUPCAKE TIME YET?

OOH!

WHAT'S THE GOLDEN STUFF?
PINEAPPLE. THESE ARE PINEAPPLE UPSIDE-DOWN CUPCAKES.

WHERE DO YOU GET ALL THESE AMAZING CUPCAKE IDEAS?
IT'S MY MOM, MOSTLY. SHE'S CUPCAKE-OBSESSED.

MY MOM IS SHOPPING-OBSESSED!
MY MOM IS CLEANING-OBSESSED!

MY MOM SAYS SHE HAS NO TIME FOR HOBBIES BECAUSE OF ME AND MY BROTHERS.
SHE HAS THREE BROTHERS.

I'LL BRING MORE CUPCAKES IN WHENEVER MY MOM AND I MAKE MORE.
SO, EVERY DAY?

THAT'S CUPCAKE OVERLOAD. MAYBE YOU COULD BRING SOME IN EVERY FRIDAY?
INSTEAD OF TACO TUESDAYS, WE'LL HAVE CUPCAKE FRIDAYS!

I GUESS THIS MEANS WE'RE FRIENDS.
YEAH, WE CAN DO THAT!

NICE TO SEE YOU ON TIME, MISS BROWN. NOW, EVERYONE, PLEASE TAKE OUT YOUR WORKBOOKS.

Dear diary,
I hope Callie means it when she says she's still my best friend.
I've known her family since before I was even born. Our moms met in cooking class while they were pregnant. Callie and I always say we have a psychic connection. That we sent each other messages in the womb. We were joking, but I sort of believed it.
And her family is like my family too. Mrs. Wilson is like my second mom. And Mr. Wilson is like my dad. And since I never see my dad, he's the closest thing I've got.
Maybe today at the barbecue, Callie will apologize. And everything will be back the way it was...
Katie

Chapter 7

THAT WEEKEND
SIZZLE
HI, KATIE-DID! I HOPE THAT IS FILLED WITH LOTS OF MY FAVORITE VANILLA CUPCAKES!
WITH VANILLA FROSTING!

SHARON! KATIE!

WHERE'S JENNA TODAY?
SHE'S WITH HER FRIENDS...
...WHEN YOU'RE SIXTEEN A FAMILY BARBECUE IS APPARENTLY A HORRIBLE PUNISHMENT.

WELL, WE'VE GOT A FEW MORE YEARS LEFT OF PEACE LEFT WITH THESE TWO, AT LEAST.

HOW DO YOU LIKE MIDDLE SCHOOL SO FAR, KATIE?

UM, IT'S ONLY BEEN TWO DAYS. IT'S KIND OF HARD TO TELL.

I'M SO GLAD THE GIRLS ARE ON THE SAME BUS ROUTE. MIDDLE SCHOOL CAN BE PRETTY SCARY.
IT'S NICE THAT THEY HAVE EACH OTHER TO NAVIGATE THROUGH IT.

CALLIE TOLD ME SHE'S BEEN WALKING TO SCHOOL. AREN'T YOU TWO WALKING TOGETHER?

IT'S NO BIG DEAL. I LIKE TO TAKE THE BUS, AND CALLIE LIKES TO WALK.

CALLIE NEVER MENTIONED IT TO ME!

HEY, FOOD'S NOT GOING TO BE READY FOR ANOTHER HALF HOUR.
I PUT UP THE VOLLEYBALL NET IN CASE YOU GIRLS WANT A REMATCH AFTER LAST YEAR'S CRUSHING DEFEAT TO YOUR MOMS.
KIDS SERVE FIRST!
WHOMP

WHOOSH!
WHOMP
LOOKS LIKE YOU GIRLS WIN!
I CAN'T BELIEVE IT, CONSIDERING I'M THE WORST VOLLEYBALL PLAYER EVER!
FOOD'S READY!
KATIE, REMEMBER THAT TIME YOU ATE SIX PIECES OF CORN ON THE COB?
WELL, NOBODY STOPPED ME!

I CAN'T BELIEVE WE WEREN'T PAYING ATTENTION. SIX PIECES!
AND I DIDN'T EVEN GET A STOMACHACHE!

WANT TO GO TO MY ROOM?
SURE!

I MIGHT EAT ALL THE CUPCAKES WHILE YOU'RE GONE!

WHEN DID SHE START LIKING VAMPIRE BOYS?

YOU'VE GOT TO SEE MY PICTURES FROM CAMP. I HAVE SO MUCH TO TELL YOU.

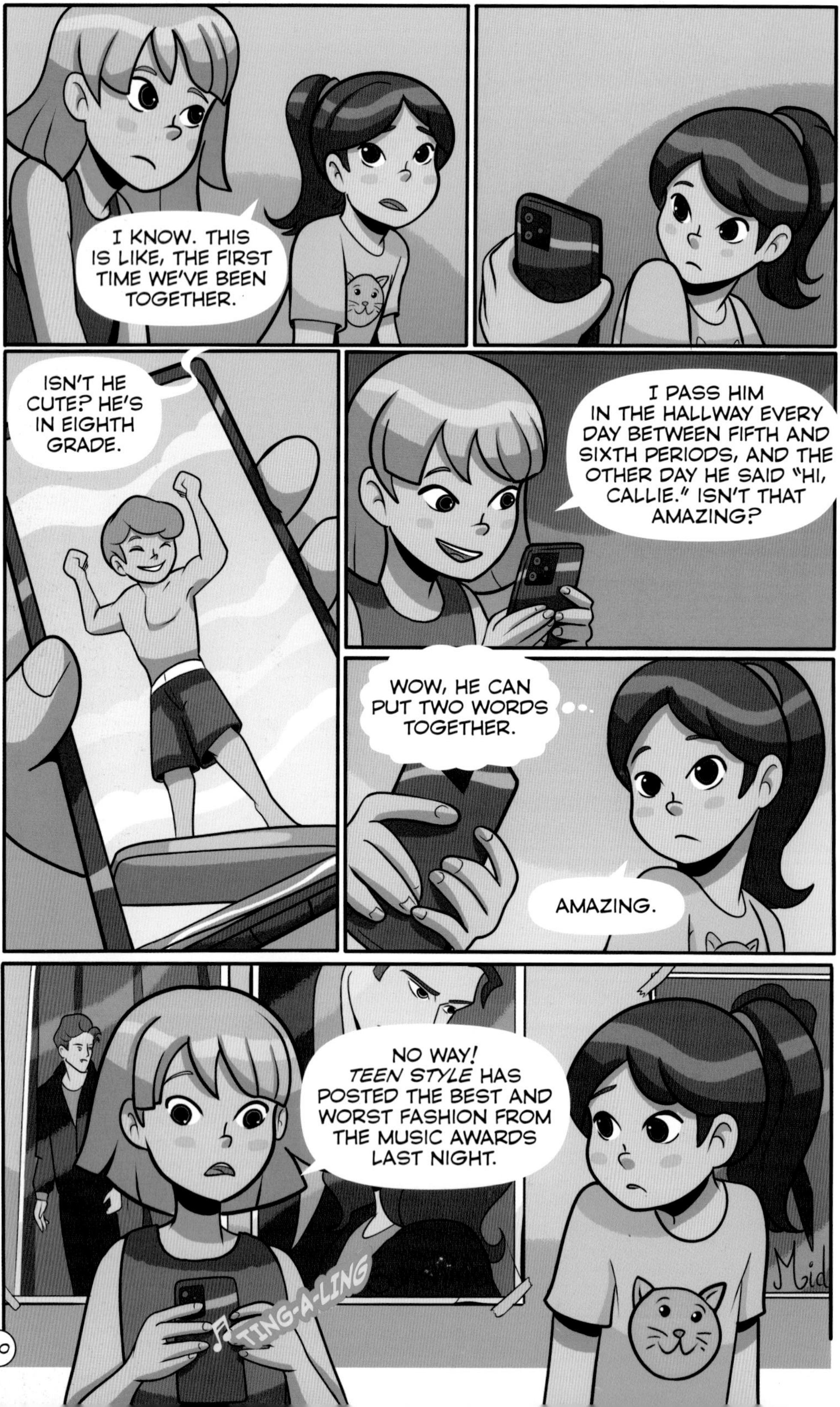

I KNOW. THIS IS LIKE, THE FIRST TIME WE'VE BEEN TOGETHER.

ISN'T HE CUTE? HE'S IN EIGHTH GRADE.

I PASS HIM IN THE HALLWAY EVERY DAY BETWEEN FIFTH AND SIXTH PERIODS, AND THE OTHER DAY HE SAID "HI, CALLIE." ISN'T THAT AMAZING?

WOW, HE CAN PUT TWO WORDS TOGETHER.

AMAZING.

OH MY GOSH, THAT DRESS IS THE ***WORST***!
YAWN

HEY, CALLIE.
YEAH?

THE OTHER DAY YOU SAID WE WERE STILL BEST FRIENDS. I'M JUST WONDERING ABOUT THAT. I MEAN... BEST FRIENDS SIT TOGETHER AT LUNCH. THEY TALK TO EACH OTHER DURING SCHOOL.

I KNOW WHAT I SAID. IT'S COMPLICATED. I STILL WISH WE COULD BE BEST FRIENDS, BUT...
BUT WHAT?

YOU'RE STILL MY FRIEND, KATIE. YOU'LL ALWAYS BE MY FRIEND.

JUST NOT BEST FRIENDS.

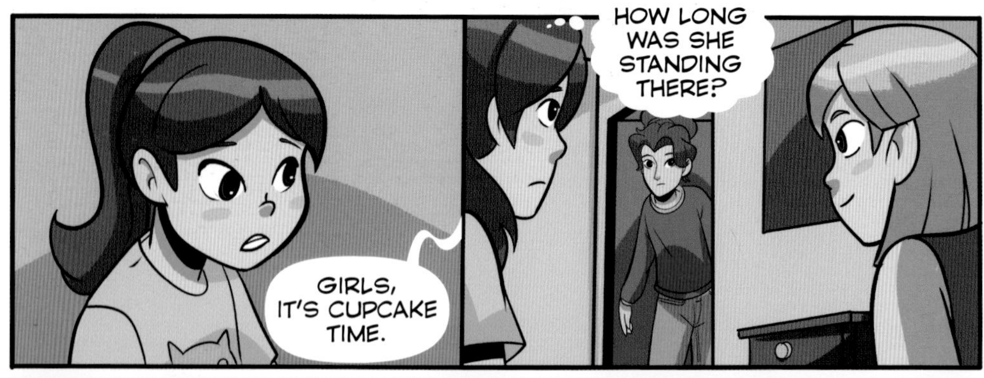
GIRLS, IT'S CUPCAKE TIME.
HOW LONG WAS SHE STANDING THERE?

Chapter 8

TUESDAY
DID YOU HAVE A NICE TIME AT YOUR DAD'S?
YEAH, WE WENT TO MY FAVORITE SUSHI RESTAURANT.

HOW WAS CALLIE'S?

PRETTY MUCH WHAT I EXPECTED, I GUESS.
YOU OKAY?

I THINK SO. RIGHT NOW, I'M MOSTLY STRESSED ABOUT GYM.
ME TOO. THE UNIFORM SHORTS ARE SO BOXY AND BAGGY.

FOR SURE. ALSO, I STINK AT SPORTS.

IN MY OLD SCHOOL WE DIDN'T HAVE TO TAKE GYM. WE COULD TAKE YOGA OR DANCE.

GOOD THING I DIDN'T WEAR MY UNICORN UNDERWEAR TODAY.
PARK STREET
SIXTH PERIOD
PARK STREET
GRUNT
THEY'RE GOING TO HURT SOMEBODY!
I HAVE THREE BROTHERS. I'M USED TO IT.
PARK STREET

LINE UP IN ROWS FOR ME, PEOPLE! WE DON'T DO ANYTHING IN THIS CLASS WITHOUT WARMING UP!
PARK STREET
PARK STREET
GOOD EFFORT! NOW I'M GOING TO SPLIT YOU UP INTO TEAMS FOR VOLLEYBALL.
PLEASE LET ME BE ON A TEAM WITH EMMA. PLEASE LET ME BE ON A TEAM WITH EMMA...
PARK STREET
PARK STREET
PARK STREET
PARK

WHAT ARE YOU WAITING FOR?

NICE SERVE!

UH-OH, FRONT ROW...

WHOMP!

TAP

OOF!

KATIE, YOU LOOK LIKE THAT SPRINKLER IN MY BACKYARD, SILLY ARMS. THE ONE WITH ALL THOSE ARMS THAT WAVE AROUND AND SPRINKLE WATER EVERYWHERE!
HA-HA
GEORGE IS MY FRIEND, SO I KNOW HE'S ONLY TEASING, BUT...
HEY, DO YOU WANT SILLY ARMS ON YOUR TEAM? WE'LL TRADE HER.
YEAH, WE'LL NEVER WIN WITH THIS ONE ON OUR TEAM.

HEY, SILLY ARMS!

WHAT'S THAT ABOUT?

GYM CLASS. WE WERE PLAYING VOLLEYBALL, AND GEORGE SAID MY ARMS LOOK LIKE THE SILLY ARMS SPRINKLER.

THAT'S SO MEAN!

BUT IT'S TRUE. I THINK I HATE GYM NOW.

WEIRD QUESTION, BUT DO YOU KNOW THE *TEEN STYLE* WEBSITE?

YEAH, IT'S THE BEST!

HEY, WHY DON'T YOU TAKE THE BUS HOME WITH ME TODAY? WE CAN CHECK OUT THE WEBSITE IF YOU'RE CURIOUS.

THANKS! I'LL TEXT MY MOM.

Not until I talk to Mia's parents. We'll arrange something for another day.

NOT TODAY. MOM WANTS TO CALL YOUR MOM.
HOW AM I SUPPOSED TO MAKE NEW FRIENDS IF MOM WON'T LET ME?

IT'S OKAY— MY MOM IS THE SAME WAY. HERE'S MY NUMBER. YOUR MOM CAN CALL TONIGHT. MAYBE WE CAN DO IT TOMORROW.

SHE IS SO COOL ABOUT EVERYTHING... WHY CAN'T I BE THAT WAY?

Chapter 9

THE NEXT DAY
HER FRONT YARD IS MUCH NEATER THAN MINE. NO DANDELIONS...
THAT'S MILKSHAKE AND TIKI. IF YOU DON'T LIKE DOGS, I CAN PUT THEM IN A CRATE.
NO, I LOVE DOGS! I WANT ONE SO BAD, BUT MOM'S ALLERGIC. CAN I PET THEM?
SURE!
YIP! YIP!
FOLLOW ME.

MOM, CAN YOU PLEASE TELL DAN TO TURN DOWN THE MUSIC?

OH, HELLO, MIA. AND THIS MUST BE KATIE.

NICE TO MEET YOU.

WOULD YOU MIND ASKING HIM YOURSELF? I'VE GOT A VIDEO CONFERENCE IN ABOUT THREE MINUTES.

YOU KNOW HE WON'T LISTEN TO ME.
PLEASE GET A SNACK FOR YOU AND KATIE, TOO!

MOM USED TO WORK AT A FASHION MAGAZINE IN NEW YORK, BUT THEN SHE MET EDDIE, WHO LIVES HERE.
SO WE MOVED HERE, AND NOW SHE WORKS OUT OF THE HOUSE. SHE'S STARTING HER OWN CONSULTING BUSINESS.
KEEP OUT
THIS IS DAN'S ROOM! HE'LL BE MY STEPBROTHER WHEN MOM AND EDDIE GET MARRIED IN A FEW MONTHS.
TOO LOUD?
WHAT DO YOU THINK?

MY OLD ROOM IN MANHATTAN WAS SO MUCH NICER. CAN YOU BELIEVE THOSE FLOWERS? I THINK SOME OLD LADY MUST HAVE LIVED IN HERE BEFORE.
EDDIE KEEPS PROMISING THAT WE'LL PAINT IT, BUT HE AND MOM ARE ALWAYS SO BUSY WITH WEDDING PLANS AND STUFF.
SHE CALLS HER ALMOST-STEPDAD BY HIS FIRST NAME?
YOU WANT TO CHECK OUT *TEEN STYLE*?
SURE.
IT'S FUN. THEY HAVE A WHOLE SECTION OF CELEBRITY PHOTOS, AND YOU CAN RATE THE OUTFITS THEY'RE WEARING.
WHAT DO YOU THINK?
IT'S NICE, I GUESS. I MEAN, IF SHE LIKES IT, THAT'S WHAT'S IMPORTANT, RIGHT?
I THINK IT'S TOO LONG. TAKE A FEW INCHES OFF THE BOTTOM, AND IT WOULD BE PERFECT. SEVEN!

LOVE THE COLOR OF THIS ONE! NINE!
SHE'S REALLY INTO THIS STUFF.

THIS IS *REALLY* FUN. YOU CREATE AN AVATAR OF YOURSELF, AND THEN YOU GET TO TRY ON DIFFERENT OUTFITS TO SEE HOW THEY WOULD LOOK. I'M GOING TO MAKE ONE FOR YOU!
MEDIUM HEIGHT... BROWN EYES...WAVY BROWN HAIR...
THIS LOOK IS VERY COSMOPOLITAN. WHAT DO YOU THINK?

I DON'T REALLY LOVE WEARING SKIRTS...

WANT TO PLAY WITH THE DOGS?
YES!!

THEY'RE AMAZING!
BUZZZZ
MOM'S ON HER WAY TO PICK ME UP.
SO SOON? TOO BAD. BUT MAYBE YOU CAN COME OVER AGAIN SOON.
OR YOU CAN COME OVER MINE.

Chapter 10

THURSDAY NIGHT
YOU SURE YOU DON'T NEED HELP, KATIE?
NO THANKS, I'VE MADE THIS RECIPE A MILLION TIMES.
CHOCOLATE CUPCAKES
1 1/2 cups flour
1 cup sugar
1/3 cup unsweetened cocoa
2 eggs
2 teaspoons vanilla extract
RECIPES ARE AMAZING. IF YOU FOLLOW THE DIRECTIONS EXACTLY, YOU CAN MAKE SOMETHING COMPLETELY AWESOME.
THERE SHOULD BE A RECIPE FOR MIDDLE SCHOOL.
Mix together 1 evil locker, 1 confusing best friend, 3 mean girls, 1 strict math teacher, 2 silly arms
MAYBE NOT *THAT* RECIPE.

KATIE
EMMA
MIA
ALEXIS
ARE THESE THE GIRLS YOU EAT LUNCH WITH?
YEP.

YOU FORGOT ONE.
I HOPE SHE DOESN'T MEAN CALLIE...
OKAY IF I DECORATE ONE FOR EVERYONE WHO WORKS IN MY OFFICE?
SURE, I'LL HELP. WE CAN BOTH DO CUPCAKE FRIDAYS.
FRIDAY
IT'S CUPCAKE FRIDAY!
WHAT KIND ARE THEY?
I ASKED KATIE ON THE BUS, BUT SHE WOULDN'T TELL ME.
I MADE CHOCOLATE CUPCAKES BUT MADE THE ICING DIFFERENT COLORS JUST FOR FUN.

THEY LOOK SO GOOD. I WANT TO EAT MINE RIGHT NOW!
I LIKE TO SAVE THE BEST FOR LAST.
KATIE
EMMA
MIA
ALEXIS
COME ON, LET'S GET IN LINE!
YOU REALLY COULDN'T WAIT, COULD YOU?
WHO MADE UP THE RULE ABOUT EATING DESSERT AFTER A MEAL, ANYWAY?
THIS IS SO GOOD, KATIE. YOU COULD BE, LIKE, A PROFESSIONAL BAKER.
THANKS, BUT I DON'T REALLY KNOW HOW TO DO ANYTHING FANCY, LIKE—
YOU WILL NOT BELIEVE WHAT THOSE SO-CALLED POPULAR GIRLS JUST DID! EMMA AND I WERE WAITING IN LINE, AND MARCUS RIDGLEY WAS STANDING IN FRONT OF US, AND SYDNEY CAME UP WITH THOSE OTHER GIRLS...
...AND SYDNEY WAS LIKE, "HEY, MARCUS, WE'RE BEHIND YOU, OKAY?" AND THEN THEY CUT RIGHT IN FRONT OF US!
RIGHT IN FRONT OF US.
DID YOU SAY ANYTHING?
WELL, NO, BUT WHAT'S THE POINT?

IT'S NOT LIKE THEY WERE GOING TO MOVE. THEY THINK BECAUSE THEY'RE IN SOME CLUB, THAT GIVES THEM SPECIAL PRIVILEGES OR SOMETHING. IT'S ANNOYING! I CAN'T STAND THEM!

SHE MEANS CALLIE, TOO.

ALEXIS, KATIE'S FRIEND IS ONE OF THEM.

I KNOW. I'M SORRY. CALLIE WAS NICE AT CAMP. MAYBE YOU GET BRAINWASHED OR SOMETHING WHEN YOU JOIN THE POPULAR GIRLS CLUB.

NOT *ALL* CLUBS ARE BAD. AT MY OLD SCHOOL WE HAD A FASHION CLUB, AND A CLUB FOR KIDS WHO LIKE MOVIES. STUFF LIKE THAT.

THAT MAKES SENSE. THOSE CLUBS ARE ABOUT SOMETHING REAL. NOT SOMETHING MADE-UP, LIKE BEING POPULAR.

YOU KNOW WHAT WOULD BE THE COOLEST CLUB EVER? A CUPCAKE CLUB! YOU DON'T HAVE TO BE POPULAR TO JOIN. YOU JUST HAVE TO LIKE CUPCAKES.

NOW THAT'S A CLUB I WOULD LIKE!

THE CUPCAKE CLUB. IT SOUNDS LIKE FUN.

WE SHOULD TOTALLY DO IT.

REALLY? I WAS MOSTLY KIDDING.

NO, REALLY, WE SHOULD TOTALLY DO IT. THIS SCHOOL NEEDS MORE CLUBS.

WE COULD HAVE OUR MEETINGS ON FRIDAYS AT LUNCH, WHEN I BRING IN CUPCAKES.

GOOD IDEA, EXCEPT I'VE NEVER MADE A CUPCAKE BEFORE IN MY LIFE.
NOT EVEN FROM A MIX?
WE ALWAYS GOT THEM FROM THE BAKERY DOWN THE STREET. THEY WERE SOOOOO GOOD.
BUT OURS WILL BE BETTER. ALTHOUGH I DON'T HAVE A LOT OF BAKING EXPERIENCE EITHER. I KNOW MINE WON'T BE AS GOOD AS YOURS, KATIE.
IT'S EASY. YOU JUST HAVE TO FOLLOW A RECIPE...

YOU SHOULD ALL COME TO MY HOUSE THIS WEEKEND. WE CAN HAVE A CUPCAKE-MAKING SESSION!
A CUPCAKE LESSON? THAT SOUNDS LIKE FUN.
I JUST NEED TO ASK MY MOM. I'LL TEXT EVERYONE TONIGHT, OKAY?
I'M SO EXCITED!
DEFINITELY!
SURE!
CALLIE LOVES TO BAKE. CAN I REALLY START A CUPCAKE CLUB WITHOUT ASKING HER TO JOIN?

Dear diary,
Mia, Alexis, and Emma are my friends. I'm so glad I met them all. Because without them, I'd have nobody!
I still haven't told Mom about what happened between me and Callie. I'm not sure why. I feel like maybe she'll be disappointed in me. Or maybe I don't want to say it because I don't want it to be true.
I really like my new friends, but I'm still so sad about losing Callie.
Katie

Chapter 11

FRIDAY
SO HOW MANY GIRLS ARE IN THE CUPCAKE CLUB?

FOUR. ME, MIA, EMMA, AND ALEXIS.

DID YOU INVITE CALLIE TO JOIN?

I WAS THINKING ABOUT IT. I JUST DON'T... I DON'T KNOW IF SHE WANTS TO. SHE KIND OF MADE OTHER FRIENDS THIS YEAR.

IT FEELS GOOD TO SAY THAT OUT LOUD!
THAT HAPPENS SOMETIMES. PEOPLE GROW UP, AND THEY CHANGE. IT HAPPENED TO ME IN FIFTH GRADE. MY BEST FRIEND, SALLY, BECAME BEST FRIENDS WITH A NEW GIRL AT OUR SCHOOL.

I WAS REALLY, REALLY SAD, BUT THEN I MET NEW FRIENDS.

I'M SORRY THAT HAPPENED TO YOU.

THANKS.

CALLIE AND I SAID WE'D STILL HANG OUT SOMETIMES. I THINK I'LL ASK HER.

Hey, Cal. Making cupcakes tomorrow at 2. Wanna come?

CALLIE'S NOT COMING.
I'M SORRY.

I KIND OF EXPECTED IT. BUT I WOULD HAVE FELT BAD IF I DIDN'T ASK HER.

HEY, CAN I TELL THE GIRLS THAT WE'RE ON FOR TOMORROW?

SURE. I WAS THINKING WE COULD START WITH SOMETHING SIMPLE. VANILLA CUPCAKES WITH VANILLA FROSTING.

THAT SOUNDS GREAT. AND UM... WE MIGHT, YOU KNOW, NEED SOME HELP, BUT I'M THINKING THAT IF WE'RE GOING TO BE A CUPCAKE CLUB, WE SHOULD LEARN TO MAKE THEM ON OUR OWN.
I HOPE I'M NOT HURTING HER FEELINGS.

OH, OKAY! I'LL HAVE TO BE HOME, OF COURSE, TO BE THERE WHEN YOU NEED TO PUT THE CUPCAKES IN THE OVEN, BUT THAT SOUNDS RIGHT TO ME. YOU CAN JUST YELL IF YOU NEED ME.

THE NEXT DAY...

DING-DONG!

HI!

YOU MUST BE KATIE. I'M WENDY TAYLOR, EMMA'S MOM. I WAS HOPING I COULD MEET YOUR MOM.
WENDY, NICE TO MEET YOU IN PERSON. I'M SHARON. PLEASE COME INSIDE.
SORRY. MY MOM IS REALLY OVERPROTECTIVE.
I KNOW HOW YOU FEEL. MY MOM'S THE SAME WAY.

WHOA, IT'S LIKE CUPCAKE CENTRAL.

WE BAKE A LOT OF CUPCAKES, SO WE'VE GOT ALL THE STUFF.

DON'T YOU USE A MIX?

MOM SAYS IT'S EASY TO DO IT FROM SCRATCH, AND WE CAN USE BETTER INGREDIENTS.

BEFORE WE START, WE SHOULD ALL WASH OUR HANDS.

WOW, YOU ARE A STRICT TEACHER.
SPLASH!

CAN YOU IMAGINE IF MRS. MOORE TAUGHT US HOW TO MAKE CUPCAKES?

CONCENTRATION IS THE KEY TO SUCCESS IN THE CLASS, STUDENTS! WITHOUT CONCENTRATION, YOU WON'T BE ABLE TO MAKE YOUR CUPCAKES!

THAT IS TOO PERFECT. CAN YOU DO MS. BIDDLE?

WHO WANTS TO MAKE A HYPOTHESIS ABOUT HOW THESE CUPCAKES WILL TASTE?
DELICIOUS!

WAIT, I CAN DO MS. CHEN. LOOK ALIVE, PEOPLE! IT'S TIME TO MAKE SOME CUPCAKES!

I NEVER KNEW CUPCAKES WERE SO FUNNY.

YOU ARE LATE, MRS. BROWN. DETENTION!

EMMA, YOUR MOM WILL BE BACK FOR YOU AND ALEXIS AT FOUR, SO YOU GIRLS MIGHT WANT TO GET STARTED. I'LL PREHEAT THE OVEN FOR YOU, AND THEN I'LL BE IN THE DEN IF YOU NEED ME.

BASICALLY, WE JUST FOLLOW THE RECIPE. FOR CUPCAKES, YOU USUALLY MIX THE DRY INGREDIENTS TOGETHER FIRST.
YOU MEAN THE FLOUR AND BAKING POWDER AND SALT, RIGHT?
RIGHT! BUT KATIE SAID NOT THE SUGAR YET.
NEXT, YOU USE THE MIXER TO BEAT THE EGGS AND SUGAR TOGETHER.
THE RECIPE SAYS "BEAT UNTIL LIGHT AND FOAMY." IS THIS HOW IT'S SUPPOSED TO LOOK?

LOOKS GOOD TO ME! NEXT IS THE MELTED BUTTER AND VANILLA.

ADD HALF THE FLOUR MIXTURE...
WHIR!

POOF!
IS THAT FLOUR ON YOUR FACE, MISS BECKER? DETENTION!
IT'S STARTING TO LOOK LIKE BATTER NOW!

YOU HAVE TO FILL EACH UP ABOUT THREE-QUARTERS FULL OR THE CUPCAKES GET TOO BIG.
THIS ICE-CREAM SCOOP WORKS GREAT!
IT'S ESPECIALLY FOR CUPCAKES. IT SCOOPS OUT THE PERFECT AMOUNT.
THIS IS THE HARDEST PART.
IT GOES FAST IF WE MAKE THE FROSTING WHILE WE WAIT. WE JUST HAVE TO WASH OUT THIS BOWL.

SIFT THE POWDERED SUGAR INTO THE MIXER WITH THE SOFTENED BUTTER...
WHIR!
I DON'T KNOW IF THIS IS THE BEST USE OF MY SKILLS.
POOF!
I THOUGHT YOU'VE NEVER DONE THIS BEFORE?
I HAVEN'T! I GUESS I HAVE A HIDDEN TALENT FOR FROSTING CUPCAKES.
LOOK AT MY POOR, SAD CUPCAKE!

I KNOW WHAT WILL MAKE IT BETTER.

YOU'RE A NATURAL!

CAN I TRY MAKING THE CUPCAKES FOR LUNCH NEXT FRIDAY? I REALLY THINK I CAN DO IT.

SURE! YOU CAN ALWAYS CALL ME IF YOU NEED HELP.

WE PROBABLY SHOULDN'T EAT THESE BEFORE DINNER, SHOULD WE?

WELL, I THINK WE NEED TO TEST THEM OUT...FOR RESEARCH PURPOSES.

SMART THINKING!

Chapter 12

Dear diary,
This week at middle school was full of good things and bad things. It felt like I was on a middle school roller coaster!
MONDAY
CLICK!
TUESDAY
PARK STREET
DON'T PICK KATIE UNLESS YOU WANT TO LOSE!

WELL DONE, MISS BROWN.
WEDNESDAY

MRS. CASTILLO, YOU FORGOT TO ASSIGN TODAY'S HOMEWORK!
THURSDAY

THANKS, TEACHER'S PET!

LEAVE HER ALONE.

FRIDAY
TA-DA!

OOH, THEY LOOK SO PRETTY!

I HOPE THEY TASTE GOOD. WE DIDN'T HAVE ANY VANILLA, AND I THINK I PUT IN AN EXTRA TEASPOON OF SALT BY MISTAKE.

LET THE SECOND MEETING OF THE CUPCAKE CLUB BEGIN!

CUPCAKE CLUB? ARE YOU SERIOUS? WHAT IS THIS, THIRD GRADE?
YEAH, THAT'S SO LAME!

NOT AS LAME AS THE POPULAR GIRLS CLUB.

EXCUSE ME? DID YOU SAY SOMETHING?

I CAN BRING SOME EXTRA CUPCAKES FOR YOU TO TRY NEXT TIME.
SHE NEVER LETS ANYBODY GET TO HER!

NO THANKS.

WELL, THAT WAS FUN.

WHO WANTS A CUPCAKE?
THOSE GIRLS ARE SO COOL...JUST LIKE MIA...
WHAT IF MIA GETS BORED WITH THE CUPCAKE CLUB? WHAT IF SHE FINDS OTHER FRIENDS?
THERE'S NO USE IN WORRYING ABOUT WHAT *MIGHT* HAPPEN. CONCENTRATE ON HOW THINGS ARE NOW.

BOOP
Can u come over for dinner tomorrow night? Indian food! Nom nom! 😋

Chapter 13

MONDAY
GOOD MORNING, STUDENTS! YOUR HOMEROOM TEACHERS WILL BE DISTRIBUTING PERMISSION SLIPS FOR THE FIRST DANCE OF THE YEAR.

THIS YEAR'S DANCE WILL BE BIGGER THAN EVER. THAT AFTERNOON, WE'LL BE HOLDING A SPECIAL FUNDRAISING EVENT FOR THE SCHOOL. CHECK YOUR FLYER FOR DETAILS.

I ALWAYS HEARD WE HAD DANCES IN MIDDLE SCHOOL. I JUST DIDN'T THINK IT WOULD BE SO SOON.

DO YOU THINK WE ACTUALLY HAVE TO *DANCE* AT THE DANCE? BECAUSE MY DANCING SKILLS ARE ABOUT THE SAME AS MY VOLLEYBALL SKILLS.

WE HAD DANCES AT MY OLD SCHOOL. SOMETIMES PEOPLE DANCED. MOSTLY EVERYONE JUST HUNG AROUND AND TALKED.

DID BOYS AND GIRLS DANCE TOGETHER?
SOMETIMES.

DID YOU SEE THE PART ABOUT THE FUNDRAISER? IT'S GOING TO BE IN THE PARKING LOT OF THE SCHOOL. IF YOU HAVE AN IDEA TO MAKE MONEY FOR THE SCHOOL, YOU CAN SET UP A BOOTH.

YEAH, IT SAYS THE BOOTH THAT MAKES THE MOST MONEY WILL GET A PRIZE.

I HEARD THE BASKETBALL TEAM IS DOING A DUNKING BOOTH WITH ALL THE GYM TEACHERS. I BET THAT WILL MAKE A LOT OF MONEY.

MAYBE WE COULD HAVE A DUNKING BOOTH FOR MATH TEACHERS.
OUR CLUB IS GOING TO HAVE THE BEST BOOTH AT THE FUNDRAISER!
THAT'S WHY WE HAVE TO KEEP IT TOP SECRET.
ONLY SYDNEY CAN TURN A GOOD CAUSE INTO SOMETHING ABOUT HERSELF.
RIGHT, BUT I WONDER WHAT THEIR TOP SECRET IDEA IS?

YOU KNOW, I BET WE CAN RAISE A LOT OF MONEY SELLING CUPCAKES. WHO COULD SAY NO TO A CUPCAKE FOR A GOOD CAUSE?

THERE ARE ABOUT FOUR HUNDRED KIDS IN THE SCHOOL. LET'S SAY HALF OF THEM GO TO THE DANCE. THAT'S TWO HUNDRED.

DON'T FORGET TEACHERS AND PARENTS AND YOUNGER BROTHERS AND SISTERS. THAT COULD BE ANOTHER TWO HUNDRED PEOPLE, FOR A TOTAL OF FOUR HUNDRED. NOW LET'S SAY THAT HALF THOSE PEOPLE BUY CUPCAKES—

WE'D NEED TWO HUNDRED CUPCAKES.

THAT SOUNDS LIKE A LOT OF CUPCAKES.

IT'S ABOUT SEVENTEEN DOZEN. WE COULD BAKE A FEW DOZEN AT A TIME OVER FOUR OR FIVE DAYS. SINCE IT'S FOR THE SCHOOL, I BET WE CAN ASK OUR PARENTS TO DONATE THE INGREDIENTS.

IF WE SELL EACH CUPCAKE FOR FIFTY CENTS, WE'D MAKE A HUNDRED DOLLARS!

FIFTY CENTS? AT THE CUPCAKE SHOP IN MANHATTAN, THEY CHARGE FIVE DOLLARS A CUPCAKE. THE CUPCAKES WE'VE BEEN MAKING ARE ALMOST AS GOOD.

WHO WOULD PAY FIVE DOLLARS FOR ONE CUPCAKE?

MAYBE WE COULD CHARGE TWO DOLLARS A CUPCAKE.

THAT WOULD WORK. IF WE SOLD ALL THE CUPCAKES, WE'D MAKE FOUR HUNDRED DOLLARS. WE MIGHT EVEN WIN THE CONTEST.

WE SHOULD DEFINITELY DO THIS!

I'M SURE THIS IS BETTER THAN WHAT THE "POPULAR GIRLS" ARE PLANNING.

IF WE WIN... MAYBE CALLIE WILL REALIZE SHE'S IN THE WRONG CLUB.

I'M IN. NOW WE JUST NEED ONE THING.
WHAT?

A PLAN!

Chapter 14

SATURDAY
IT WAS NICE OF YOUR PARENTS TO LET US DO A PRACTICE BAKE TODAY, ALEXIS.
AS LONG AS WE CLEAN UP THE MESS, THEY'LL BE OKAY!
REMIND ME WHAT WE ADDED IN THESE AGAIN?
CHOCOLATE CHIPS, MINI MARSHMALLOWS, AND SPRINKLES.
I CAN'T WAIT UNTIL WE FROST THEM. WE SHOULD DO A TASTE TEST *WITHOUT* FROSTING, DON'T YOU THINK?
GOOD, BUT MESSY!

MMMMM...

TOO SWEET!
I DON'T THINK SO.

WE NEED TO TEST THESE ON SOME POTENTIAL CUSTOMERS.

ALEXIS SAYS YOU NEED SOME CUPCAKE TESTERS?
THEY'RE NOT FROSTED YET. THEY'LL PROBABLY BE SWEETER WHEN WE ADD THE FROSTING.

THEY'RE VERY SWEET ALREADY.

THEY'RE TASTY, BUT I'M NOT A BIG FAN OF MARSHMALLOWS. YOU KNOW WHAT MAKES ME HAPPY? A PLAIN VANILLA CUPCAKE.

JUST LIKE CALLIE'S DAD...

MRS. BECKER, MAY I PLEASE HAVE TWO BOWLS?

MAKE THAT ONE BLUER.

NOW JUST IMAGINE THERE ARE PLAIN VANILLA CUPCAKES INSIDE.

THEY'RE JUST RIGHT!

I BET YOU'LL SELL A HUNDRED OF THOSE.

Chapter 15

EIGHT DAYS BEFORE THE DANCE
OKAY, I'VE MADE A CHART OF OUR BAKING PLAN.

DATE/SUPPLIES/DOZENS
TUESDAY/Katie/
WEDNESDAY/Alexis/
THURSDAY/Emma/
FRIDAY/Mia/
SATURDAY/KAEM (frosting)/
ALL THE BAKING WILL BE DONE AT KATIE'S HOUSE.

AND WE'LL TAKE TURNS BRINGING SUPPLIES. SATURDAY WE'LL ALL BRING STUFF TO MAKE THE FROSTING.

IT TAKES A LOT LONGER TO BAKE CUPCAKES THAN I THOUGHT.
HA-HA!

YOU'RE DOING A BAKE SALE FOR THE FUNDRAISER? NOW *THAT'S* REALLY ORIGINAL.
BAKE SALES ARE SO BORING!

YOU KNOW WHAT'S BORING AND UNORIGINAL? FOLLOWING SYDNEY AROUND AND REPEATING EVERYTHING SHE SAYS LIKE A PARROT.

EVERYBODY LIKES CUPCAKES. WHAT'S THE POPULAR GIRLS CLUB DOING?

IT'S TOP SECRET. NOBODY HAS EVER DONE WHAT WE'RE PLANNING. WE'RE GOING TO BLOW EVERYONE AWAY.
NOT EVERYONE.

I WONDER WHAT THEY'RE PLANNING? I BET IT'S REALLY GOOD.

I BET THEY HAVEN'T EVEN THOUGHT ABOUT IT YET. OTHERWISE, THEY'D BE BRAGGING ABOUT THEIR IDEA TO EVERYONE.
YOU'RE PROBABLY RIGHT.

TUESDAY BEFORE THE DANCE
BAKING MEASUREMENTS ARE TRICKY. MY ADVICE: DON'T QUADRUPLE THE RECIPE. MAKE ONE BATCH AT A TIME. THEN YOU'LL END UP WITH PERFECT CUPCAKES. I KNOW YOU CAN DO IT! NOW HOW ABOUT A HUDDLE?

GOOOOO, CUPCAKE CLUB!

I THINK WE SHOULD DIVIDE UP THE WORK BASED ON OUR STRENGTHS. I'LL DO THE MEASURING. KATIE, YOU'RE OUR BEST EGG CRACKER...

FIRST DOZEN DOWN!

DO WE REALLY HAVE TO FREEZE THEM?
THEY'LL STILL TASTE GREAT. IT'S THE BEST WAY TO KEEP THEM FRESH FOR SATURDAY.

TIME TO JUMP IN THE SHOWER, KATIE.
YOU'LL HAVE TO DRAG ME.
HMM. MAYBE ALL THIS CUPCAKE BAKING IS TOO MUCH FOR YOU.
NOPE, IT'S FINE!

How to Make 200 Cupcakes:
1. Do homework in a dentist office
2. Eat dinner
3. Clean up after dinner
4. Make four dozen cupcakes
5. Clean up after making cupcakes
6. Shower
7. Rinse
8. Sleep
9. Repeat
10. Repeat
11. Repeat

Chapter 16

FRIDAY EVENING
ARE YOU SURE WE SHOULD BE DOING THIS? IT'S GOOD THAT WE HAVE ALL THE CUPCAKES MADE, AND I'M GLAD WE GOT TO BAKE RIGHT AFTER SCHOOL.
BUT WE STILL HAVE TO FROST ALL THE CUPCAKES, AND...
WE'RE GOING TO FINISH TOMORROW MORNING. THERE'S STILL A DANCE AFTER THE FUNDRAISER, AND YOU NEED A DRESS!
I MEAN, I DON'T REALLY *NEED* A DRESS, DO I? IT'S NOT LIKE SOME FANCY DANCE. AND YOU KNOW, JEANS ARE THE WAY I EXPRESS MYSELF.
TRUE. I DON'T WANT TO MAKE YOU DO SOMETHING YOU DON'T WANT TO DO. BUT I JUST WANT TO SHOW YOU THAT DRESSES CAN BE FUN.

SO, WHAT SHOP ARE WE GOING TO FIRST?
MOM, SERIOUSLY?

I PROMISED MRS. BROWN I'D STICK WITH YOU GIRLS.

BESIDES, YOU'RE LUCKY TO HAVE AN EXPERT FASHION CONSULTANT TO HELP YOU SHOP.
COME ON, THERE'S A GREAT SHOP AROUND THE CORNER!

THIS IS SO CUTE. YOU SHOULD TRY THIS ON!

I DON'T KNOW. IT'S BLACK. BLACK CLOTHES REMIND ME OF VAMPIRES.
OKAY, SO YOU LIKE BRIGHT COLORS. WHAT ELSE DO YOU LIKE?
I DON'T KNOW. I DON'T KNOW WHAT'S IN STYLE AND WHAT'S NOT. WHEN I GO SHOPPING WITH MY MOM, I JUST GET JEANS AND THEN PICK OUT WHATEVER SHIRTS I LIKE.
YOU CAN DO THAT WITH A DRESS, TOO. JUST LOOK AROUND AND SEE WHAT YOU LIKE.

I LOVE THE COLOR. AND IT LOOKS GOOD ON THE MANNEQUIN. SHE DOESN'T HAVE A HEAD, THOUGH, SO MAYBE ANYTHING WOULD LOOK GOOD ON HER.
NO, I LIKE IT! TRY IT ON!
KATIE, COME OUT! I'M DYING TO SEE HOW YOU LOOK!
OOH, IT'S PERFECT! SPIN FOR ME.

YOU HAVE TO GET IT! YOU COULD EVEN WEAR SNEAKERS IF YOU WANT WITH IT, AND IT WILL LOOK SO CUTE.

THAT DRESS IS GROSS, MAGS. I WOULDN'T WEAR THAT TO GYM CLASS.
SYDNEY?!

ISN'T IT A LITTLE TOO EARLY FOR HALLOWEEN, KATIE?
KNOCK IT OFF, SYDNEY.

I CAN'T LET MIA FIGHT ALL MY BATTLES.

NO, IT'S OKAY. WHAT EXACTLY DO YOU MEAN, SYDNEY?

WELL, THAT'S A GRAPE COSTUME, ISN'T IT? NO WAIT— YOU'RE THAT PURPLE DINOSAUR.

YOU KNOW, SYDNEY, VIOLET WAS A HOT RUNWAY COLOR THIS FALL. I WAS JUST READING ABOUT IT IN THE COLOR TRENDS COLUMN IN *FASHION WEEKLY*.

VIOLET OR NOT, IT'S AN UGLY DRESS.

I DON'T CARE IF *YOU* THINK IT'S UGLY. I LIKE IT!

Chapter 17

SAY "CUPCAKE"!

CUPCAKE!!!

cupcake

GIRLS SOCCER
TEAM SELFIE
STATION

Chess Club
Bake Sale
OH NO! A BAKE SALE!

WELL, THEY DON'T HAVE PARK STREET MIDDLE SCHOOL CUPCAKES LIKE WE DO.
AND THEY HAVE MOSTLY COOKIES, AND THEY'RE CHARGING ONLY FIFTY CENTS FOR THOSE.

IS THAT THE POPULAR GIRLS CLUB BOOTH?

PGC
Makeover
Magic

THE PGC MIGHT HAVE MUSIC AND FLYERS AND GLITTER, BUT WE HAVE DELICIOUS CUPCAKES. LET'S GO WIN THIS!

cupcake
2$

MRS. MOORE?

HELLO, MISS BROWN. IT MUST HAVE BEEN A LOT OF WORK TO MAKE ALL THESE CUPCAKES.

THERE ARE MORE IN BOXES. WE MADE TWO HUNDRED. WELL, TWO HUNDRED AND FOUR, ACTUALLY. THAT'S SEVENTEEN DOZEN.

I'LL TAKE ONE, PLEASE.
VANILLA! MY FAVORITE.
OUR FIRST SALE!
WOOT!
I'LL TAKE A BLUE ONE.
YELLOW, PLEASE.

HI,
LUCY.

I KNOW.
IT'S TERRIBLE,
ISN'T IT? AND IT
COST ME FIVE
DOLLARS!
GASP!

I THOUGHT
IT WOULD BE FUN,
BUT THIS IS JUST
TOO MUCH. IT'S MORE
MAKEOVER *TRAGIC*
THAN MAKEOVER
MAGIC.

CAN YOU AND
ALEXIS HANDLE THINGS
FOR A MINUTE? WE'LL
BE RIGHT BACK.
MAYBE
LUCY JUST GOT
UNLUCKY. IT LOOKS
LIKE THEY'RE DOING
GREAT.

I DON'T KNOW MUCH ABOUT FASHION, BUT THAT DOESN'T LOOK RIGHT TO ME.
THAT SHOULDN'T LOOK RIGHT TO ANYBODY.

HEY, KATIE! DO YOU WANT A MAKEOVER?
I DON'T WEAR MAKEUP, SORRY. YOU SHOULD COME CHECK OUT OUR CUPCAKE TABLE. I BET YOUR DAD WOULD LIKE ONE. THEY'RE VANILLA.
DID YOU MAKE THE CUPCAKES WITH THE SCHOOL COLORS?
YES, I—I MEAN, *WE* DID. WE HAVE A CLUB. THE CUPCAKE CLUB.
THEY WERE BEAUTIFUL AND DELICIOUS. MADE FROM SCRATCH, I COULD TELL.
I WOULD LOVE TO HIRE YOU TO MAKE SOME FOR THE PTA LUNCHEON THIS SPRING. WE'D PAY YOU, OF COURSE.
MOM! THE CUPCAKE CLUB IS A *RIVAL* BOOTH! YOU'RE CONSORTING WITH THE ENEMY.

IT'S JUST A CUPCAKE.

Chapter 18

HEY, MIA! HOW DID THE CUPCAKE SALES GO?

NOT BAD, MR. VALDES. WE HAVE ONLY SEVENTEEN LEFT.

TELL YOU WHAT. I'VE GOT A BIG MEETING ON MONDAY. I KNOW EVERYONE AT WORK WOULD LIKE SOME CUPCAKES. I'LL TAKE EVERYTHING YOU HAVE LEFT.

THAT WILL BE THIRTY-FOUR DOLLARS, PLEASE.
THANKS, EDDIE. YOU DIDN'T HAVE TO DO THAT.
I DID. I'M MAKING EVERYONE WORK LATE, AND THEY DON'T KNOW IT YET.

SEE YOU AT
THE DANCE!

MY BABY'S
FIRST DANCE.
YOU LOOK SO
BEAUTIFUL!

MO-OM!

YOU BOTH LOOK SO NICE!
SO DO YOU TWO! WHAT'S TO EAT?

PUNCH, VEGGIES, AND A LOT OF CUPCAKES.
I DON'T THINK I CAN LOOK AT ANOTHER CUPCAKE TODAY.

I CAN ALWAYS LOOK AT A CUPCAKE. EVEN IF IT CLEARLY HAS FROSTING FROM A CAN, LIKE THIS ONE.

SPEAKING OF CUPCAKES, I TALKED TO MY PARENTS ABOUT THE PTA CUPCAKE ORDER. YOU KNOW, THEY'RE ACCOUNTANTS, SO THEY CAN HELP US FIGURE OUT WHAT TO CHARGE SO WE CAN MAKE A PROFIT. THEY SAID THEY COULD EVEN SET US UP AS A BUSINESS IF WE WANT.

THEN THE CUPCAKE CLUB IS OFFICIALLY OPEN FOR BUSINESS!

THOSE CUPCAKES YOU MADE WERE SOOOOO GOOD.

WERE THEY HARD TO MAKE?

IT'S EASY. YOU JUST FOLLOW THE RECIPE.

HEY, I LOVE THIS SONG!
HEY, SILLY ARMS!

NOW IT'S TIME TO ANNOUNCE THE WINNERS OF OUR FIRST CONTEST. THE WINNING TABLE TODAY RAISED FOUR HUNDRED AND EIGHT DOLLARS FOR OUR SCHOOL. LET'S HEAR IT FOR THE CUPCAKE CLUB!

GASP!

SQUEE-EEEE!

WE DID IT!

YES!

DEEJAY, DROP ME A BEAT!
KATIE, CONGRATULATIONS!
LOVE YOUR DRESS!
LOVE YOURS, TOO!
COME DANCE WITH US.

NO, I HAVE TO...I'LL CALL YOU TOMORROW, OKAY?
OKAY.
HEY, CALLIE! I'M GLAD WE'RE FRIENDS!
ME TOO!

NEW Recipe for
Middle School
Mix together:
1 purple dress
1 corny mom
204 cupcakes
3 new friends
1 old friend
Stir gently till they're
all blended together.
Then dance.

Here's a sneak peek of the next

CUPCAKE DIARIES

book:

Mia in the Mix

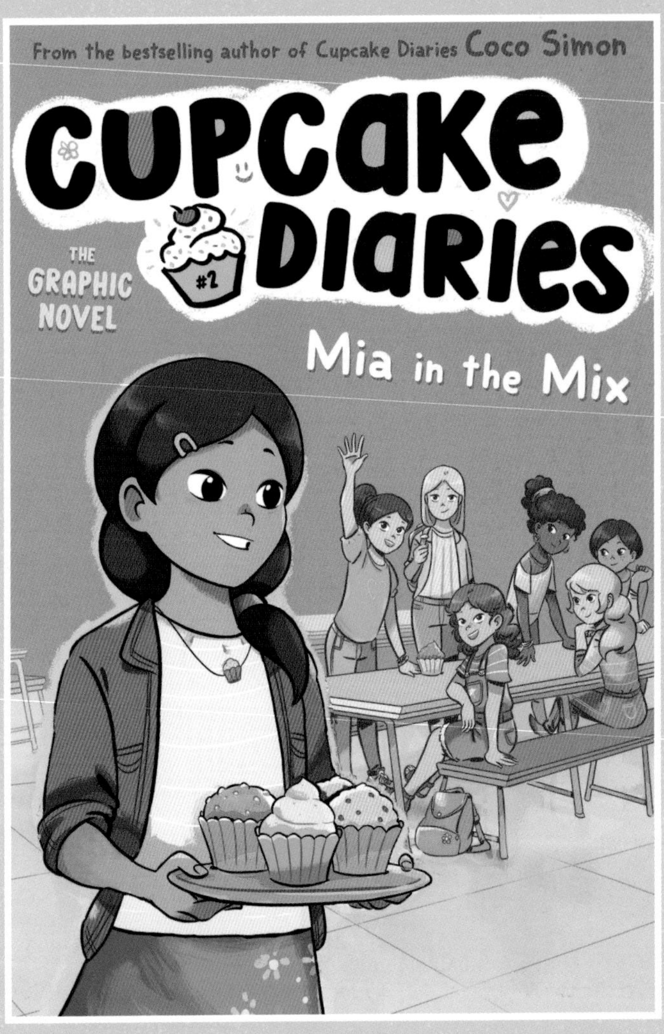

Katie Brown
Mia Vélaz-Cruz
Emma Taylor
Alexis Becker
SALE

Chapter 1

I STILL CAN'T BELIEVE THAT WE SOLD ENOUGH CUPCAKES TO WIN THE FUNDRAISER!
I CAN! OUR CUPCAKES WERE AWESOME.

USING THE SCHOOL COLORS REALLY MADE THEM STAND OUT.

WE SHOULD ALL WEAR THE SHIRTS THAT WE WON TO SCHOOL ON MONDAY.

THAT'S A NICE IDEA.
YEAH, WE WORKED HARD ON THOSE CUPCAKES. WE SHOULD SHOW OFF THAT WE WON!

THAT'S MY MOM. SEE YA!
BEEP!
HOW WAS THE DANCE?
IT WAS FUN. AND THE BEST PART IS THAT THE CUPCAKE CLUB WON THE FUNDRAISING CONTEST.
THAT'S GREAT, HONEY!
IT FEELS PRETTY GOOD TO WIN. I NEVER WON ANYTHING AT MY OLD SCHOOL IN MANHATTAN. THAT SCHOOL WAS SO COMPETITIVE!
I TOLD YOU THERE WOULD BE ADVANTAGES TO MOVING TO THE SUBURBS.
ONE ADVANTAGE DOESN'T ERASE A HUNDRED NEGATIVES.
MY POOR DAUGHTER. SORRY I MENTIONED IT.

LOOK AT THIS SCHOOL SWEATSHIRT. WE WON THEM AS PRIZES, AND THE CUPCAKE CLUB WANTS TO WEAR THEM ON MONDAY.

HOW NICE.

NO, NOT NICE! SWEATSHIRTS DON'T LOOK GOOD ON ANYONE. IF I WEAR THIS, I'LL LOOK LIKE A BOILED DUMPLING.

MIA, I'M SURPRISED. YOU'VE ALWAYS BEEN GREAT AT TRANSFORMING YOUR OLD CLOTHES INTO NEW CREATIONS. REMEMBER HOW MUCH YOU HATED YOUR SCHOOL UNIFORM AND HOW YOU ACCESSORIZED IT? I'M SURE YOU CAN DO SOMETHING WITH THIS SWEATSHIRT.

MAYBE TOMORROW. GOOD NIGHT, MOM!

SUNDAY
WHIRRP
PS

MONDAY MORNING...
HEY!
OH NO! DID YOU FORGET TO WEAR YOUR SWEATSHIRT?
I AM WEARING IT. WHAT DO YOU THINK?
COOL! DID YOUR MOM DO THIS?
I DID.
WOW, THAT'S AWESOME. THAT MUST BE HARDER TO DO THAN MAKING CUPCAKES.
IT JUST TAKES PRACTICE.
BURRRRRPPPPPP!
GROSS!

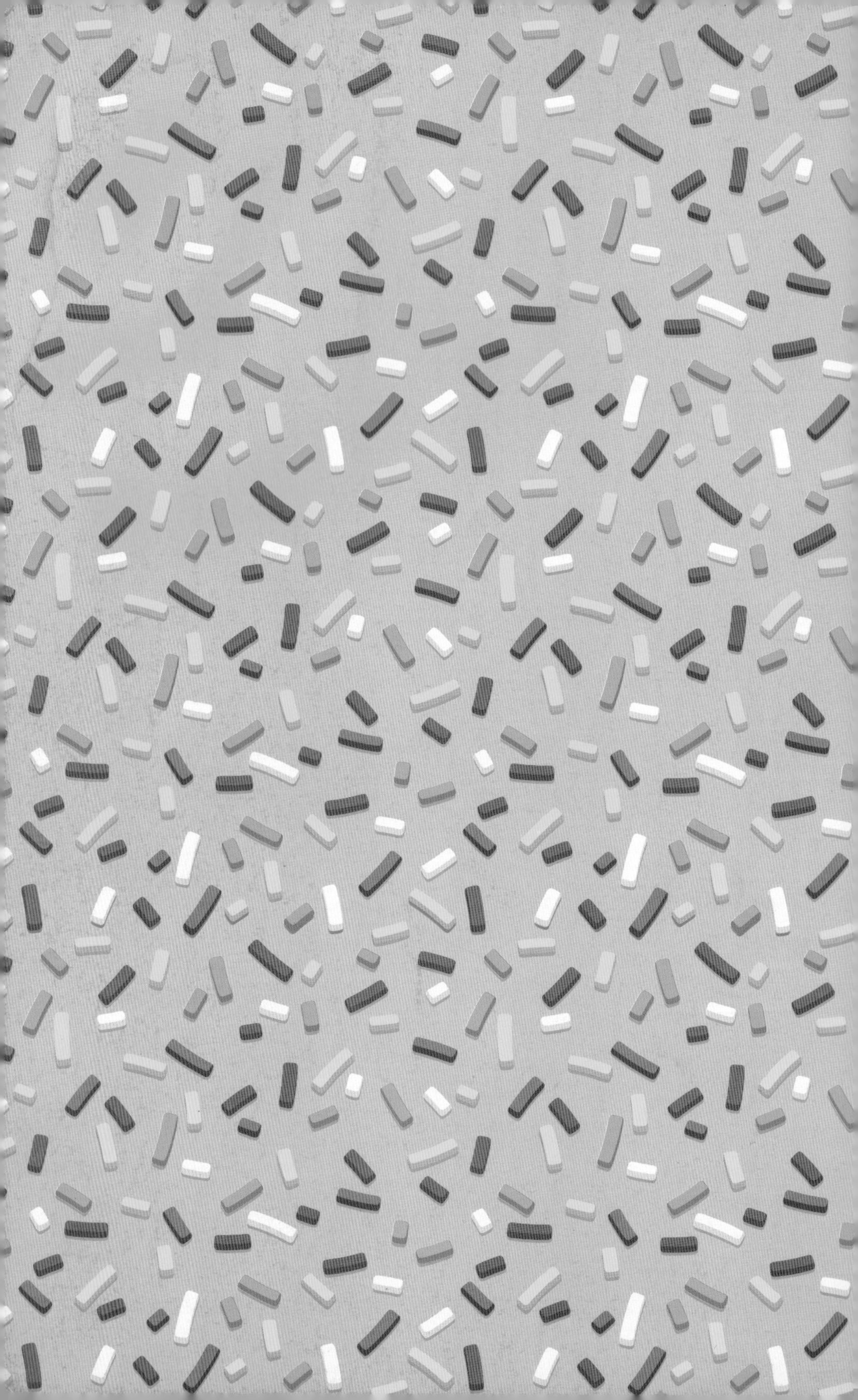

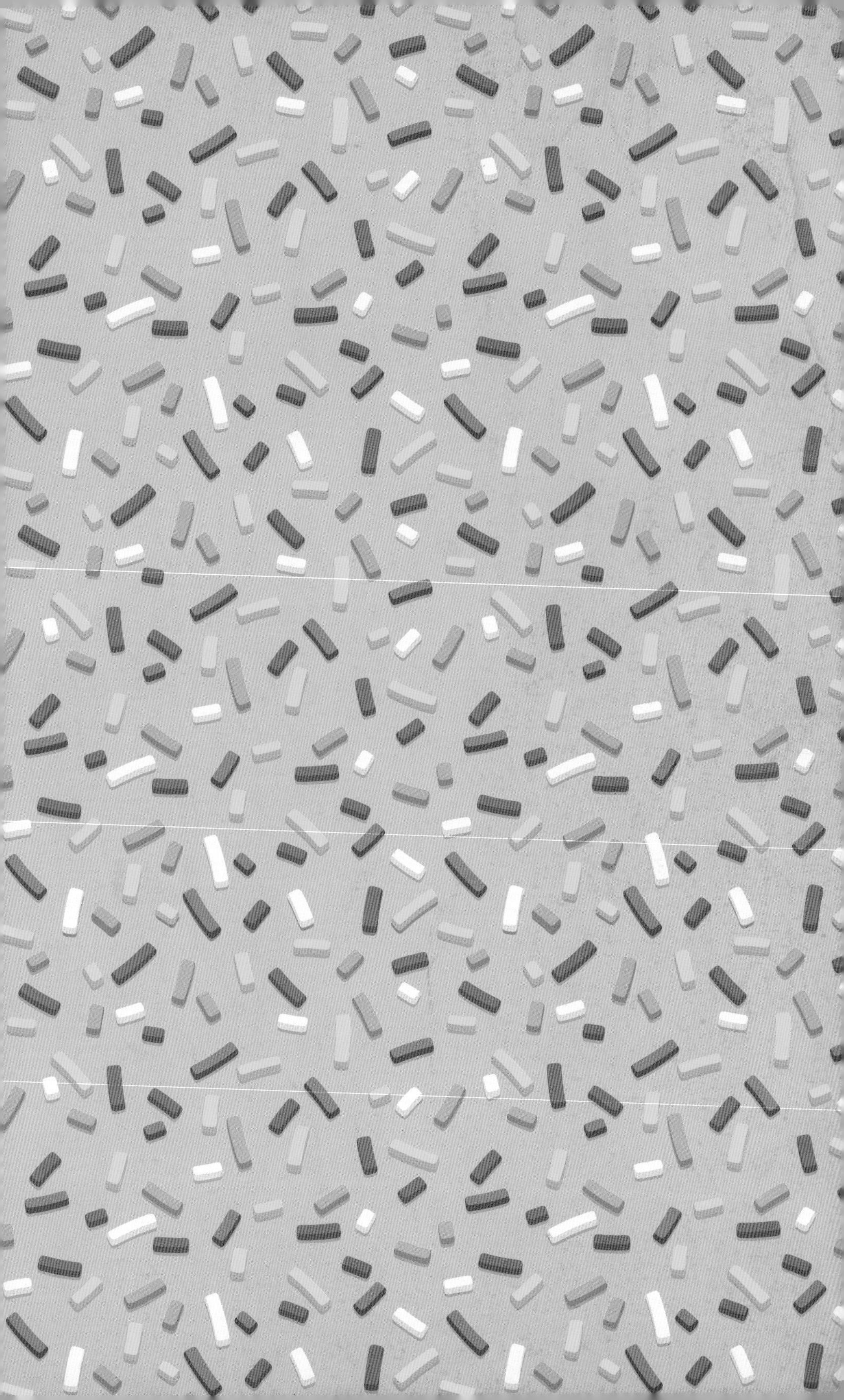

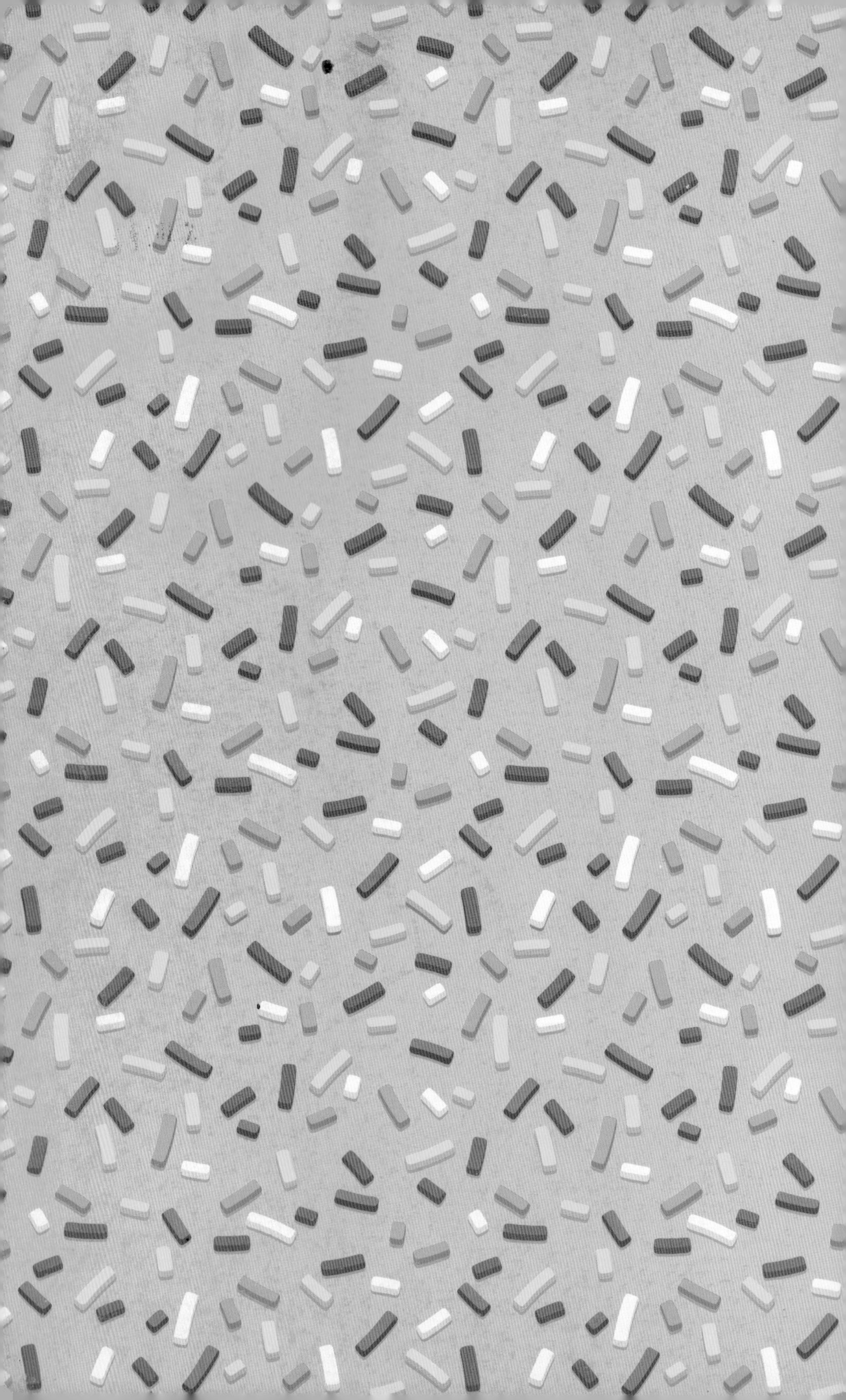